BAREFOOT BOOKS

The barefoot child symbolises the human being whose natural integrity and capacity for action are unimpaired. In this spirit, Barefoot Books publishes new and traditional stories whose themes demonstrate the pitfalls and dangers that surround our progress through life; the qualities that are needed to face and overcome these dangers; and the equal importance of action and reflection in doing so. Our intention is to present stories from a wide range of cultures in such as way as to delight and inspire readers of all ages while honouring the tradition from which the story has been inherited.

In memory of Helen Luke

Barefoot Books Ltd
PO Box 95
Kingswood
Bristol BS15 5BH

Designed by Design/Section
Printed in Singapore

ISBN 1 898000 84 0

THE SECRET RIVER

An African Myth

retold by Laurens van der Post and illustrated by Larry Norton

BAREFOOT BOOKS

BATH

At a certain time, in a certain place by the river, there was a girl who was very beautiful. Her beauty was so great that it was spoken of in other places in the long, long ago, and she was called many different names. But it was really one and the same girl, living at this place by the river.

All the other girls in the kraals around became very jealous of her. Although she did everything she could to try and please the women of her place, they only became more and more jealous of her.

So they secretly made a plan between themselves, and in the early morning, when all the women would go down to fetch water by the river in the cool of the day, they went very early without telling her, and took off all their beads and jewellery and hid them in the sand behind some dense bushes.

When the girl appeared at last, and was surprised to find the others already there, they called out to her: 'You, who are always so proud and look at us from a great distance, look at what we've done! We have thrown all our jewellery away into the river – and you must do the same!'

Larry Norton 95 ©

So, seeing how hostile they were and anxious to be their friend, she took off all her jewellery and threw it into the river.

The moment she had done so all the other girls started dancing with joy, saying to her with scorn: 'You are as stupid as you claim to be beautiful,' and they went behind the bushes and came back with their jewellery and held it out mockingly for her to see.

Devastated by what she had done, the girl put down her urn and went to the river and cried: 'Oh river, you who flow by so gently, have you seen my jewels?'

Larry Norton.

But the river merely murmured: 'Pass on, young lady. Pass on.' So she went along the river bank and asked the same question again and again, and always there came just the same answer from the water: 'Pass on, young lady. Pass on.'

At last, in desperation, she came to a very deep pool, so deep that it was almost black in the middle, and she called out: 'Oh pool in this river, have you seen my jewels?' And from the pool there came a strange, commanding voice, which answered: 'Enter!'

She obeyed, and went down and down and down, and came to the bottom of the pool where the light was like twilight, and there she was confronted by one of the ugliest and most repulsive old ladies that you could imagine.

The old lady had only one leg, and one arm, and her body was covered with large sores. She hopped about on one leg in front of the girl crying: 'You who are so young and beautiful. Laugh at me! Go on, laugh at me!'

But the girl, instead of laughing, was so overcome by the horror of the old lady's plight that tears came into her eyes. The old lady, noticing this, said to her in a more appealing voice: 'Come and lick my sores.' The girl's heart was so tender that she overcame her horror and licked the sores of the old lady.

Then the old lady said to her: 'Oh, you are as loving as you are beautiful, and as a reward I shall protect you. I live here with a horrible monster. He has gone out for the day to seek human beings to devour. You will know when he is coming back because all of a sudden a little wind will blow, a few drops of rain will fall, and then it will be as dry and hot as before, and the monster will appear. So, eat the food here that I have cooked for him, and when you have finished eating you must hide yourself in my secret place behind this wall.'

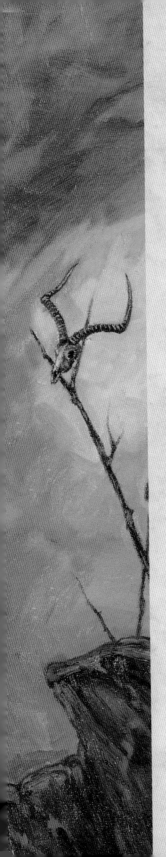

The girl had hardly finished eating and hidden herself, when there came one of those funny little winds that appear all over that part of Africa when there is a great drought and the wind will not bring the clouds together but blows them apart. A few drops of rain fell, then it became as dry and hot as before, and the monster appeared. He looked terrifying, with strange long hair, a red mouth and teeth like a wild boar.

Immediately, the monster felt that there was something wrong and ran about the house, sniffing and watering at the mouth, calling out that he smelt a human being. He looked all over the place, getting more and more angry and insisting: 'I smell a human being! I am hungry and I must eat!'

The old lady replied soothingly: 'There is no human being here. You may kill me, but you will find no human being.'

The monster was so hungry – because his hunting for food had been unsuccessful – that he thought seriously about eating the old lady, but he did not do so because if he had eaten her, he would have had no-one to cook for him.

Accepting at last that there was no human to eat, he went to sleep so that he could set out early in the morning to look for food.

Before the Morning Star – 'the Foot of the Day' as it was called in those parts – appeared, he was up and out looking for human beings to eat. The old woman then took the girl out of her hiding place and said: 'You of the heart of love, I shall now reward you.'

She took out a large pot of the finest hippopotamus fat and anointed the girl's head all over with it. She put some wonderful brass rings on her legs, and bracelets on her arms, and gave her anklets of the most beautiful coloured beads.

She dressed her in a new apron made out of the softest skin of a young female duiker, which had a hem sewn with copper thread, and a shawl for her shoulders made of jackal skins, fringed with the skin of a young silver-maned jackal.

Finally, she gave the girl a small round stone and explained: 'This round stone is the most important of all. Take it carefully with you and when you come out of the river and stand again on the earth, take the stone and rub it well underneath your armpits, and then walk on home. Be very careful not to look back. But do not go so far that you cannot do what I tell you now, as the most important thing of all.'

'Rub the stone again under your armpits and, without looking back, throw it over your shoulder into the pool so that it can come back to me. Walk on, but still do not look back until you meet someone who will offer you water to drink. If you do all these things I have told you, I shall see that my monster does not catch you. Go in peace, you dear, kind girl, and may the rain always fall upon you.'

The girl did as she was told. She took particular care to rub the round stone twice under her armpit, because she knew from all the stories of the people of long, long ago that the armpit is the place closest to the source of life in the human being. Then she threw the stone across her shoulder, and heard a tiny splash to show that she had thrown it correctly.

Then she walked back to the place where she had thrown her jewellery into the river. There she found her younger sister waiting for her. The younger sister was overcome with joy, and told her that everybody had been looking for her everywhere, and had been dismayed and terribly upset because they had not been able to find her. Everybody had become afraid that some wild animal had eaten her or, even worse, that Tokoloshe, the dreaded water spirit who chased young girls, had caught her.

Larry Norton. 95

'Please know how we have missed you,' said her sister, 'and looked for you everywhere over and over again. But you must be very tired. Please come and sit beside me and have some of this water I have just fetched from the river to drink, and tell me what happened to you.'

The girl drank and told her story, then the two sisters went on home together.

    As they came near the village, a little girl saw them and ran among the kraals crying out the news that the girl had been found. All the women came out and everybody crowded round her, asking questions and wanting to know where she had been. As always, she was truthful and told them all that had happened to her.

Well, of course you know what human beings are. Some people were very pleased at her good fortune, but others were more jealous than ever, saying: 'How like her to have such luck. If it had been any one of us, none of these things would have happened.'

The children of her uncle, who was a wicked man, were more jealous than ever, and in their greed they ran off to the river and followed it along to the pool. There the voice of the old lady called to them. They entered and they too came to the bottom of the pool.

When they saw the old lady and she said to them, as she had said to their cousin: 'Laugh at me! Go on, laugh at me!' they laughed at her; and when the old lady begged them to come and lick her sores, they said: 'You hideous old thing, do you think we would do anything as unpleasant as that, for you?'

So the old lady did not hide them. A light wind blew, a few drops of rain fell, it became hot and dry as before and then the monster appeared. He exclaimed: 'Aha! I smell good human flesh to eat!'

The old lady not only had not hidden them, but did nothing to help them, and the monster ate well.

Afterword

For centuries, this story has been told in spoken form in many places in the interior of Africa – on the plains, in the deserts and in the bush. Wherever a story was told, the storyteller would say to the people gathered around the fire, as he brought the story to its end: 'And then, out of the dark there appeared an enormous elephant with a very long trunk!', and then he would blow out the fire.

I have related the story here as I would have told it to a company by the fire in the bush of Africa. To me, it is unique among African tales because it is almost an allegory of the way the predominantly male cultures of the world developed with a profound unawareness of the caring and feminine values of life. I first encountered the story as a child. As I grew older, I came to consider the timeless feminine and masculine values in life more consciously and in doing so I found more and more meaning in the story.

The Secret River is my own title, and is intended to reflect the way in which rivers house secrets of great importance to the people who live close by them in the natural world. My heartfelt thanks are due to Larry Norton, who was inspired by his local river, the Musengezi, in painting the beautiful series of illustrations that accompany this retelling.

Laurens van der Post

London 1996